DRAGONLYST

a short novel

a Prologue to
THE DRAHIAD CHRONICLES

RANDALL SEELEY

All Rights Reserved

Copyright © 2014 by Randall Seeley

First Paperback Edition: March 2014

This is a work of fiction and all characters, places, and events are fiction. Any resemblance to actual persons, living or dead, is completely coincidental. The Author holds exclusive rights to this work. Unauthorized duplication is prohibited.

For More Information
www.randallseeley.com

ISBN-13: 978-1496096418
ISBN-10: 149609641X

For Mom and Dad,

Who would always stay up late and listen to my wild stories

DRAGONLYST
a short novel

CONTENTS

DRAGONLYST..1

EXCERPT FROM DRAGON BORN............85

ABOUT THE AUTHOR............................99

OTHER BOOKS BY RANDALL SEELEY.....101

CONNECT WITH ME...............................103

DRAGONLYST

I still remember the first time I witnessed a dragon transformation. To this day I can't decide what was more horrific—watching my friend's body be viciously transformed into a dragon or knowing that I was the one who was responsible. I had to do what I did. How was I supposed to know of the consequences that would follow? I just pray that one day I can figure out how to break the curse that is now flowing through our veins.

JEFRIE DANGLON GRASPED the wooden handle resting on the edge of the pitch-black cauldron, the bowl of the spoon submerged in a boiling green liquid that was filling the room with a foul odor. Sweat trickled down his forehead as the heat from the popping bubbles rose toward him.

"Careful, Danglon," a crackly voice breathed into his ear. "If your sweat drips into the dragonlyst it will throw off the balance of the chemicals and everything in here will explode—including us."

"I know, Master Kloin," he said quietly as he concentrated. *Whispering that into my ear isn't helping any* he thought to himself, but he knew Kloin was right. He had to remove his sweat. Carefully, he steadied the wooden spoon with one hand, then reached up with the other and wiped away the beads of sweat. Risking a glance at his glove, he made sure the drops were absorbed, and then quickly brought his hand back to the handle.

"Well done," Kloin commended.

Focusing back on his task, Jefrie stirred the contents while continuously checking an hourglass on the worktable beside him. Judging from the falling sand, he knew there was only about one more minute before he needed to add the final ingredient.

"Watch the timer," he heard Kloin instruct.

"Or in other words, wait for about—yes—twenty-five more seconds before I put in the astercaea?" he asked, raising an eyebrow at his master.

A smile from his master encouraged him. Jefrie knew he was talented and knew he was probably the best dralchemist apprentice in all of Ardonor, but he still enjoyed being validated every once in a while.

He watched the hourglass intently, noticing each grain of sand trickle steadily through its neck, until finally the sand crossed the forty-five minute mark. Without hesitating, he reached down and grabbed a glass beaker that contained dozens of minced pieces of astercaea, and dumped the contents into the cauldron.

As soon as the particles hit the swirling liquid, a cloud of smoke erupted into the air. Jefrie turned his head aside, forcing himself not to cough in reaction, and continued to stir. He threw the empty beaker to the side and grabbed the spoon with both hands, stirring vigorously as the beaker shattered on the ground.

"The congelation has begun, continue to stir!" Kloin encouraged.

Jefrie felt sweat reform on his forehead, but this time he ignored it. He only had a small window of time to finish the congealing before the substance cooled and coagulated.

His arms began to burn as he continued to stir, and then suddenly another cloud of smoke erupted from the semisolid contents of the cauldron.

"Dragon's blood, I did it!" he shouted as he witnessed the climax of the recipe. The substance completely solidified, and then a moment later, disintegrated into a fine silvery dust that settled to the bottom of the cauldron.

He felt a clap on his shoulder and was greeted by a smiling Kloin. Though his master's skin was wrinkly with age, Jefrie saw a deep look of approval. "Well done, Danglon, well done! Dragonlyst! And by yourself from start to finish. You just might be the best apprentice I've ever had."

"Of course I am," Jefrie said with a wink.

"We'll see," Kloin responded. "But you aren't finished yet. Add the dragonlyst dust to wine," he instructed as he handed Jefrie a measuring spoon.

Jefrie accepted the measuring spoon, and then looked down at the silvery dust at the bottom of the cauldron. *One spoon of dragonlyst dust to one two-ounce vial of wine, the last step.* Before scooping the dust into the spoon, he pointed at a set of vials that rested on the worktable next to him and motioned for Kloin to begin filling them.

"Two ounces of wine in each vial, Master," Jefrie instructed. He saw another smile appear on his master's face.

Once Kloin finished filling the vials, Jefrie began his part. He reached into the cauldron and scooped enough dust to fill the spoon, and then carefully began removing it from the cauldron. Though the dralchemy process was complete, dragonlyst dust was volatile, and he knew that any collision would cause the dust to lose its potency. *Just can't hit the cauldron* he repeated in his mind.

His hand trembled as he navigated the spoon out of the cauldron and toward the wine. *Steady hand* he thought as he reached up with his other hand to try and provide support. *If I drop it now, I'll never hear the end of it.*

"Relax Danglon, just bring it over to this vial and pour it in," Master Kloin instructed as he placed a funnel over the closest vial.

Jefrie wanted to respond sarcastically but decided against it. He took a deep breath to try and calm his nerves and then stepped forward until the spoon was positioned over the funnel. *Here goes nothing* he thought as he twisted his wrist.

He watched as the dust slowly trickled into the wine and began to interact. At first, the dust appeared to resist becoming one with the wine, but as he gently grabbed the vial and gave it a small shake, the dust began swirling until it completely disappeared. The dralchom was complete.

He couldn't contain his smile any longer as he realized what he had done. He had created dragonlyst, the catalytic dralchom used to commence or accelerate dragon transformation.

"I did it," Jefrie said with a smile. "I just made dragonlyst!"

"That you did, Danglon. Well done," Master Kloin congratulated. "Now finish the other nineteen and then we can celebrate."

Let me celebrate a little bit at least Jefrie thought as he moved back to the cauldron and started the process again. He was surprised how fluid he was now that he knew he could do it, and a short time later, he found himself pouring the last of the dragonlyst dust into the twentieth vial. Finished, he and Master Kloin grabbed corks and began stopping the vials to keep the contents from spilling.

"Now you can celebrate," Master Kloin said as he pushed a cork into the final vial.

"I have to admit, I am pretty excited that I just —"

A knock sounded on the upstairs door and Jefrie quickly cut off what he was going to say as he glanced at Master Kloin, who raised an eyebrow in concern. Master Kloin instinctively reached inside his robes, grabbing what Jefrie knew was the hilt of a dagger laced with poison. Jefrie only needed to see the dagger used once to know how deadly that poison could be—dralchoms weren't the only thing dralchemists could create.

"Do you think it's the Order?" Jefrie whispered to his master.

Master Kloin shook his head, "Arthur would have given us warning. No, I think he is letting us know that someone awaits—probably your uncle at that. It's about time for his appointment if I'm not mistaken."

It is about that time Jefrie thought as he exhaled in relief while silently scolding himself for getting tense. *Though Master Kloin did grab his dagger* he justified. But the emotions did confirm one thing about his chosen profession—brewing illegal dralchoms came with consequences, chief of which was constant paranoia.

To confirm that everything was fine, a moment later the door opened slowly and a bushy head of red hair popped through, followed by a lanky form. "Pardon the interruption, but the profound and elegant Mr. Danglon has arrived, on time as usual!" he announced with a slight bow.

Jefrie tried not to roll his eyes as he looked at his best friend. "You couldn't just say my uncle has arrived, Arthur? You have to go about using profound, and elegant, and bowing, and what not?" he asked.

"Your uncle deserves respect, Apprentice, and as guardian of this establishment, not only will I protect it, but I will announce—"

"Enough," Master Kloin interrupted, his glare mixed into his wrinkly skin. "With all the bickering you two do, I can't get anything done. Or even hear myself think! It happens all the time! It was bad enough when I had to endure my wife's bickering, but now I have to hear it from you two? What is Ardonor coming to?"

Arthur and Jefrie looked at each other and grinned.

"Maybe I should just shove you both out on the streets and be done with it. The only thing that made my wife stop bickering was her death and well, you are both young so death would do you no favors. But, well—curse the dragons—now I'm just rambling!" Master Kloin shouted while shaking his fist in the air.

Jefrie couldn't control himself any longer as a laugh escaped and Arthur followed shortly after.

"Master, you wouldn't kick me out, would you?" Jefrie asked.

"And of course not I. After all, have I ever allowed the guard to enter through these doors? Or a Templar for that matter?" Arthur asked sincerely as he unsheathed the dirk at his side and swiped it through the air.

This time it was Jefrie and Master Kloin who exchanged glances as they burst into laughter.

"As if you've ever had to resist anyone coming through those doors," Jefrie said.

At the same time Master Kloin exclaimed, "A Templar! Boy, a Templar would cut you down faster than you could reach the handle of your dirk. Now put that thing away before you hurt yourself!"

Arthur blushed and sheathed his dirk as another figure appeared at the head of the stairs.

"Templar? I'm not a Templar. I'm nearly late for my delivery because I've been standing at the cursed door! You find someone else that can deliver as well as I, Kloin? Or is it you just don't want to get paid?"

Master Kloin glared at Arthur as he grabbed the vials of dragonlyst, and then hobbled up the stairs, disappearing with Tret into Master Kloin's office. Arthur shrugged his shoulders as Jefrie gave him a scowl, and then quietly asked "what?"

"You know how my uncle is, Arthur," Jefrie said as he began walking up the stairs.

"I know, more intense than a starving man about to take his first bite!" Arthur exclaimed.

"He has to be with the schedule he has; always too busy and always another delivery. But, Tret enjoys it, and it's why he has the reputation he does. Always dependable—kind of like how I'll be when I'm a Master Dralchemist one day."

"You'll be locked up for getting caught because you won't shut your mouth about how great you are at dralchemy," Arthur retorted.

"I don't have to talk about it, the proof is in my dralchoms," Jefrie smiled back. As they reached the top of the stairs, Jefrie shut the door and locked it. Then with Arthur's help, they moved a bookshelf in front until it settled in place, completely concealing the door. *You never can be too careful in our business* Jefrie thought as he gazed at the bookshelf to ensure the door was completely hidden. Once satisfied, they moved to the front visiting room and to a stiff couch that puffed up a cloud of dust as they sat.

"Dragon's blood, does Kloin ever clean this

place?" Arthur asked as he swatted away the floating dust. "I've been sitting on this couch for several weeks and the dust doesn't seem to end!"

"Master Kloin is a good man," Jefrie replied. He knew his master was lonely. In his late seventies and a widow for the better part of a decade, the only thing keeping him alive was training Jefrie. "He doesn't have time to maintain his home."

"Cause he has you as his apprentice," Arthur teased. "If it was me he was training, he'd have plenty of time to clean, cook, and do whatever else he wanted to do to waste his time. You just don't learn as fast as I do!"

Jefrie began to respond but then heard his uncle talking from the office next door. "Shhh," he shushed Arthur, who at first began to argue with being cut off until he heard the muffled conversation as well. They didn't get to hear Master Kloin and Tret discuss business too often, but they took advantage whenever they could. After all, they knew Tret and Master Kloin were the best in the business.

"Are you sure you want to keep selling to this group? I fear they may be able to track it back to me. If the Order gets word that I'm active again..." they heard Master Kloin say.

"Trust me, Kloin, these won't get traced back to you. I have them convinced that I'm buying from several different dralchemists in Alderidon. Besides, if they get too curious, I'll just rat out Delidar Pratt—you wouldn't mind his competition conveniently disappearing would you?" Tret asked with a chuckle.

"I just don't have a good feeling about this. Can't seem to shake it!"

"Come on now, Kloin. We've been in business for the better part of fifteen years. Have I ever let you down? Ever?"

"I know, Tret. Here's what concerns me. They want it too frequently—and though I make my living doing what I love, and which also happens to be illegal—I know for a fact that this many dralchoms can't be used for any good. Weekly for the better part of three months? Asking for all of the major dralchoms? And now a steady request for dragonlyst? What are they using this for? Soon their quantity is going to rival that of the Orders!" Kloin exclaimed.

"The Orders? Come on now, Kloin. Rival the Orders? Don't you think you're being a little extreme?"

"I may be to a degree," Kloin admitted. "But I still can't reason why they need this many dralchoms. Dragonsbane I understand. But dragonshadow? And dragonlyst? What are they using it for?"

"Using it for? Who cares!"

"And the amount they are paying. It's exorbitant! I know they are paying for secrecy, but everyone who buys from anyone outside the Order pays for secrecy. They are paying for more than secrecy!"

"You are complaining about how much they pay! Who cares? Besides, they want the purest dralchoms so they pay for it. They test each batch I deliver, and are always satisfied. They pay for the quality!"

"Another reason I fear they can track it to me."

"You are good, Kloin, but so is Pratt, and Hardlin, and others."

"Then go risk your life with one of them," Kloin snapped back.

"Come on now. I won't go after this fortune without you!" Tret argued.

Kloin mumbled something under his breath.

"And you are training my nephew," Tret continued. "I wouldn't want anything other than the best for him. Think of the future this is building for him. If this continues for another three months like the contract states, we'll have enough to buy an estate! Jefrie could have his own shop hidden in the basement. Think of it. We are setting him up for success."

Jefrie tried to listen more intently as it grew quieter. He glanced at Arthur, who just shrugged his shoulders.

"All right, Tret," Kloin finally continued. "I trust you, and you are right, you've never steered me wrong. We can finish the contract. But…be careful will you?"

"That's my dear friend," Tret replied. "Now let's finish packing and I'll be on my way. Don't want to be late."

With that the conversation ended and they began to hear small clinging of glass on glass as the vials of dragonlyst Jefrie had just brewed were carefully placed into a carrying case. A moment later, the office door opened and Tret appeared.

"You lads stay out of trouble," he said as he tilted his hat. "Jefrie, I'll see you tonight," he finished as Kloin escorted him to the front door. As Kloin opened it, Tret stuck his head out, looked both ways, and then disappeared from view as he exited.

Jefrie and Arthur stood up, waiting for instructions for the next task, but as Kloin turned around Jefrie could see he was exhausted and most likely done for the day. Kloin was getting more and more tired of late.

"Jefrie, you did well today. Why don't you and Arthur have the rest of the afternoon off? Go do what other eighteen year olds do on a sunny afternoon, but be back early in the morning. We brew one of my own dralchoms tomorrow. Uses the herb flyriella. Now get out," Kloin said as he turned back toward his office.

Jefrie started to argue, but Kloin walked straight back to his office, went in, and shut the door behind him. Instead, Jefrie looked at Arthur and saw a large smile on his friend's face. Suddenly, the smile vanished.

"What is it Arthur?" Jefrie asked.

"Well, how am I supposed to get paid if I have the afternoon off?"

"Get out!" Kloin shouted from the office.

Together they looked at each other, trying their best to hold in their laughter, and then exited the house, locking the door behind them.

As Jefrie dropped his key to Kloin's house into his pocket, he looked out and saw that the streets were empty. From the position of the sun, it was late afternoon, and they only had one or two hours left before dark—enough time to go to one of the local hangouts near the docks or into the Merchant District to look at the week's wares for sale.

"Not going to lie," Arthur began, "I'm not really in the mood to just hang out today."

"I couldn't agree more, though I appreciate the time off. If I'm not mixing dralchoms, I don't really know what to do with my time anymore," Jefrie said as he kicked at the cobblestone street. "Can you think of anything to do?"

They returned to silence as Jefrie tried to think of what to do. He thought of the Palace District, *don't want to deal with nobles today*, and then he found himself thinking back to the docks. A glance at

Arthur saw a look of befuddlement on his friend's face. *No help there* Jefrie thought. *If we are going to figure out something exciting to do, I'm going to have to figure it out.*

He thought back to the dragonlyst he brewed just minutes earlier. It was his first time, and he couldn't help but replay every step in his mind. He had mastered dragonshadow a few weeks back and was practically mastering dragonsbane with how frequently they made it. But dragonlyst...*I finally did it.*

"What are you doing?" Arthur suddenly asked. "Day dreaming about dralchoms again?"

How did he know? Jefrie thought. Embarrassed that he was discovered, he quickly tried to deflect to something else, "No, fool," he began. *Think of something else!* And then it came to him. Something that was bothering him since the moment he had heard it. "I was actually wondering why Master Kloin was so nervous about Uncle Tret's route today."

"Wonder?" Arthur asked incredulously. "My mind hasn't been able to stop thinking about it. Granted, you know Kloin better than I do, but I've never seen nor heard him that anxious before. Of course I'm wondering about it!"

Jefrie nodded in agreement. *I do know Master Kloin well and I have never seen him like that.* "Something is off, isn't it?" he asked.

Arthur nodded. *I honestly wonder what is causing it?* Jefrie thought. And then he remembered what he had seen that morning just before heading to Master Kloin's.

"Arthur," he said. "I think I know of a way for us to find out."

"Find out? Find out what?" Arthur asked.

"What's making Master Kloin so nervous," Jefrie answered. "This morning I saw Tret's route."

"All right, I'm interested. What was it?" Arthur asked.

"His delivery route. The one he and Kloin were arguing about."

"Are you serious?" Arthur asked.

Jefrie nodded, remembering it clearly. "Now it's all starting to make sense," he continued. "And the best part, I know where the destination is."

"What?" Arthur asked. "Are you sure you saw the route they were discussing?"

"I'm positive. It was the only destination that didn't have the usual description of goods pinned next to it—that's what caught my attention. It's in the Merchant District, at the intersection of Denkar and Stith. Honestly only a few blocks away—if we hurry we can probably see what all the fuss was about."

"I wonder what it is?" Arthur asked, his normally

bold voice suddenly becoming slightly quieter. "Do you think it's dangerous?"

Jefrie felt a shiver go down his spine at the thought. *Kloin sure thought it was.* But there was no proof and Tret thought it was perfectly safe. But then he remembered his uncle's reaction when Tret saw Jefrie looking at his routes.

He shook his head to clear his thoughts. *I'm just letting my fancies get to me* he concluded. Then turning to Arthur he said, "Come on, it's a delivery route. Uncle wouldn't do something that dangerous. Should we go find out for ourselves?"

As Arthur nodded Jefrie opened his mouth to tell Arthur about his uncle's reaction, but then decided against it. *I'm sure Uncle yelled at me because I was snooping, not because he didn't want me to know about it* he thought.

Giving smiles of encouragement, they started making their way toward Stith Street.

Tret slipped into an alleyway nestled between two tall buildings off of Stith Street, carefully stepping around discarded rubble and trash that covered the ground. A steady creaking came from a wooden sign that swayed in a slight breeze as it tried to hang on by one rung, the paint worn off years ago. He believed this building use to be an inn, but it had been abandoned for years. Now instead of being a side entrance to an inn, it was filled with crates of garbage. *I guess I get paid enough not to complain about walking through garbage.*

He glanced around to ensure that no one was watching as he pulled his hood over his head. It was ironic to him that his clients had chosen a place near the Merchant District—which happened to be an area with the most traffic in Alderidon—and yet they asked for secrecy. *Who cares* he thought; *they pay enough for me to keep my mouth shut!*

As he started toward the door, he felt the familiar but uncomfortable flutters in his stomach. Normally, his anxiousness of having a new client would wear off after one or two deliveries, but he had been delivering here weekly for almost three months, and the feeling seemed to deepen with every delivery. *Kloin may be right.*

He rapped on the door twice, waited half a minute, and then rapped again. A moment later a voice that seemed to slither asked, "Who is it?"

"I bring a gift, not one or two, but only a gift that a dralchemist can brew," he recited as instructed.

A bolt unclasped from the other side and the door creaked open, revealing a dark stairwell that led to an upstairs attic. It was the same every time. As he stepped through the door, it slammed behind him and the bolts slid back into place. Tret tried to get a glimpse of the figure that opened the door, but as he searched he saw nothing. The uneasy feeling deepened.

He swallowed hard as he began his ascent up the stairs. Remembering his strict rules, he looked down to the steps and pulled his hood tighter around his head, blocking all of his peripheral vision. He knew what he needed to do now.

Always keep your eyes on the ground and head covered.

Never look up.

Place the dralchom onto the altar in the middle of the room.

Select one for testing and wait for inspection.

Answer any questions the Dark Lord asks.

Leave with your payment.

The rules were straightforward and direct and he knew that as long as he obeyed them, he had nothing to worry about. As he reached the top of the stairs he made sure his hood was completely covering him one more time, then reached forward and twisted the handle on the door.

As soon as the door opened he was greeted with the familiar smell of burning incense, its powerful aroma thick in the room. He instinctively gulped for air as the incense entered his lungs and caused him to cough slightly.

"He doesn't enjoy our scent," a voice in the darkness said as Tret stepped through the doorway.

Laughter followed from other voices. He felt himself flinch as the door slammed shut behind him once he entered the room.

Tret ignored the laughter as he looked at the floor in front of him. He knew his instructions, and knew which voice he needed to answer. All others he ignored. Responding to other voices wasn't in his instructions, and he didn't want to find out the consequence of violating them.

He walked toward the center of the room where a stone altar had been erected, identifiable by the flickering lights that caused shadows to dance all around the room. From what Tret could tell, the altar was the only place that was emanating any source of light, so it was easy to find—even while staring at the floor.

When he reached the altar, he knelt down and carefully pulled out the pack full of vials and set them on one of the stone shelves. He then selected one of the vials, pulled it out, and reached out his extended hand, waiting for them to take it from him.

He felt sweat trickle down his back as his anxiousness grew while he waited. It always felt like an eternity waiting for them to take the vial. His eyes flinched and his neck strained as he felt the urge to stand up and look around the room, but he forced himself to stay in the same position. Eyes down, hand extended, vial slightly grasped in his hand.

Finally a cold hand touched his own, startling him and causing him to slightly mutter—once again causing laughter to spread throughout the room. He used his senses to try to determine how many there were. There was at least one in front of him and a few on each side, but the exact number eluded him. He fought the urge to look up.

"Test the dralchom," commanded a voice Tret had heard the other refer to as the Dark Lord. He recognized it as the one he needed to obey. *It's not my business if it's a Dark Lord, an evil Lord, or any other kind of Lord.*

A second person came into view and Tret could hear an exchange as the vial was unstopped. He shut his eyes, knowing exactly what was going to happen next, and silently wished he could cover his ears. He knew what dragonlyst would do.

He heard muffled sounds of resistance as someone was dragged into the room and forced to the altar. *It might not be a someone, I'm assuming things* he tried to rationalize as he felt the person stop just a few feet from him.

He forced his eyes as tight as they could go and prayed that his ears wouldn't hear what would happen next. At first there was a shout, then a gurgle, and then the sound of choking as the person was forced to swallow the dragonlyst. Tret could hear resistance, but just like each other time, slowly the defiance ended as it was replaced with quiet sobbing. It always happened the same.

Then a scream erupted.

Tret tried to block out the noise, but could only clench his teeth tighter, his jaw beginning to hurt at the strain.

"Bring me another! She's resisting the transformation!" the Dark Lord commanded.

Tret obediently opened his eyes, blinked away a tear that had formed, and picked another vial, extending it in his hand. It was snatched much quicker and immediately brought to the victim. There was little resistance this time.

The scream grew. Tret couldn't resist any longer as he lifted his hands to his ears, trying to block out the sounds that were filling the room. The sound of flesh ripping. The sound of bones breaking. He felt a wave of heat as the transformation completed and a calm silence filled the room.

Tret shook as he continued to hold his hands to his ears. *The quiet is deceiving* he knew. He heard a pained but angry growl begin to grow from the form on the ground, and then he felt a rush as the figures in the room descended onto the helpless victim. A guttural scream cried out until it was finally silenced by the sound of steel cutting. *If Kloin knew about this part...*

"As always, Mr. Danglon, the dragonlyst you

provide is the purest, and rivals even what the Order can brew."

Tret chose to say nothing until it became awkwardly silent. All he wanted to do was calm his nerves and leave. But when no other question or comment was given, he knew he needed to respond. "It does," he said. "The best in Alderidon I hear."

"That it is," the Dark Lord said, this time only a foot or two away from him. Tret found himself flinching in spite of himself, somewhat startled that the person had come this close without him even realizing. But he was tired. His time here was finished. He had delivered his goods, witnessed horror, and was ready to leave.

"You are tense, Mr. Danglon. Do you not approve of our methods?" the Dark Lord asked with a hint of mockery.

Tret's back stiffened as his mind raced for an answer, but his head hurt, and the only thing he could hear was his heartbeat pounding in his ears.

"Answer me, Danglon. You know the rules. Do you not approve?" the Dark Lord demanded.

Tret swallowed hard and then opened his mouth. He realized how dry his tongue was as he said, "My business is to deliver goods, be paid, and then be on my way. What those goods are, or what they are used for, is none of my concern."

There was a pause that felt like eternity.

"Great answer," the Dark Lord praised.

Tret exhaled with relief despite his attempt to maintain his composure, and the mocking laughter returned. *Laugh all you want; just let me out of here!*

"One last question before you can be paid," the Dark Lord asked. "Who is your dralchemist?"

Tret felt his heart stop for a moment and his stomach leap into his throat. He knew that this question would one day come, and had prepared a false answer. But now that he was faced with the question, he felt on the verge of panic.

"It's a simple question, Danglon. Who is it? The dralchemist deserves to be recognized and rewarded. And remember, you have promised to answer me, and this is my question."

Tret knew he had to give an answer, and also knew that he would die before revealing the truth—that it was his own nephew and Kloin. He prayed his lie would be believed.

"Delidar Pratt," he answered with as much conviction as he could muster.

Silence.

Tret opened his mouth to reiterate, but shut it instead. He hadn't been asked a question, so he wasn't allowed to speak. *Let these bloody fools think on it and decide what they want* he decided.

"Pratt? I know of him," the Dark Lord finally answered. "I didn't realize he was this skilled."

Sweat trickled freely down Tret's face and he prayed that they would believe his lie. *I should have chosen Hardlin, curse me!*

"But I have been surprised before and I can be surprised again," the Dark Lord finally said. "Thank you Mr. Danglon. Your payment for twenty-four vials of dragonlyst is near the door. You are free to leave."

Tret forced himself not to exhale in relief and he quickly obeyed. He spun around and quickly started toward the exit, saw the bag of gold, and reached down and picked it up. As his hand connected, a smile appeared on his face at the pure weight of it. *It's even heavier than last time* he realized. Scooping up the coins, he started to reach for the door handle when his mind finally registered what the voice had said. Twenty-four vials of dragonlyst. Twenty-four. *We only packed twenty!*

He nearly dropped the bag of gold and it took all of his concentration not to scream out in frustration and fear as everything started to make sense. That was why the gold was heavier. That was why they had tested two vials. The order was for four more vials than usual. Tret scolded himself for forgetting such a simple detail and quickly spun around.

"I apologize," he said as he stood straight up, his hood falling from off his head. "I only brought twenty vials. I completely forgot about the extra four you ordered for this visit. But I can head straight back and get you eight more for your inconvenience, and I can promise this won't happen again!" he exclaimed.

All he saw were blank stares staring back at him and then looks of anger appearing on different faces. Unconsciously he surveyed the room. He saw twelve robed men, their heads uncovered, and their faces clearly displayed. He saw a broken and beheaded body of a woman strewn across the floor near the altar. He saw the man who stood next to the altar; his back turned at the moment, the thirteenth person. Slowly the man near the altar started to turn and Tret realized what had happened.

The rules! I broke the rules!

He locked eyes with the Dark Lord and was shocked at who he saw. He knew this man. Many people knew this man. *Dear Creator what have I gotten myself into!*

Tret tried to think of what to do and as a result quickly threw back on his hood and looked to the floor, praying inside that maybe they hadn't noticed his blunder. But he had seen their surprise fade into anger. *They know I know.* He felt himself shaking as he continued to look at the ground.

"Mr. Danglon, we accept your terms and you are free to leave. Do not let it happen again," the Dark Lord said calmly.

Tret couldn't believe his ears. *That's it? I violated the most crucial rule. I saw his face! And he's going to let me free?* But he wasn't about to argue. He quickly turned around, reached for the door, and twisted the handle.

"But you lied to us, Mr. Danglon," the Dark Lord said. "Delidar Pratt did not brew this. It was Master Kloin."

Tret's heart stopped as he froze in place.

"Now be gone," the Dark Lord continued. "I would advise you to hurry home to be with Malline, for I've heard she is lonely this night."

Each word dug deeper and deeper into Tret's soul. He knew what the message meant. Without a second thought, he pushed the door open and ran down the stairs, unbolted the outer door himself, and ran out into the street. He only had one thing on his mind. He and his wife were leaving Alderidon as soon as possible.

A sudden bang against the door startled Jefrie and it took all of his focus not to lash out and knock over the crates of garbage he was hiding behind. He glanced at Arthur and saw that his friend shared the same uneasy feeling about this place, but then breathed a sigh of relief when he saw it was Tret who was exiting the building.

"See Jefrie, everything is fine," Arthur whispered.

"No reason to be getting all jumpy!"

As if I was the only one who was jumpy! Jefrie thought. He started to smile, but then stopped. Something was wrong with his uncle. Tret stood in place, as if he was paralyzed or confused on where to go. For a moment Jefrie thought about calling to him, but then he saw a single emotion crying out from his uncle's features.

Horror.

Jefrie began to callout, but before he could form the words Tret broke into a sprint and ran out of the alleyway.

"What is going on?" Arthur whispered in his ear, his voice cracking slightly.

Jefrie almost jumped again at the noise. He didn't have an answer. His mind raced as it tried to logically process what had transpired.

"I don't know, but did you see Tret's face?" he finally asked.

"See it? Do you think I'm blind? He was terrified!"

Jefrie shook his head, hoping inside that if he denied it that it somehow wouldn't be true. *What is going on?* He wondered. He thought back to earlier that day when he overheard Master Kloin and Tret discussing this route. At the time Master Kloin was uneasy about this partnership, but Uncle Tret was adamant about it being safe, and positive that they would all benefit from it. *Maybe there is nothing to fear at all?*

Trying to calm his nerves, he whispered back, "I'm sure Tret is fine. Maybe we are just seeing things. We have been sitting behind garbage for almost an hour."

"Fine?" Arthur asked. "Do you have dragon's blood coursing through you? He looked as if he had seen a cursed dragon!" he exclaimed.

I know Jefrie thought. He tried to think of what to do. He wasn't sure where Tret had sprinted off to, but he knew he would eventually head home. "Maybe if we head back to my uncle's place," he suggested.

"You think it's safe?" Arthur asked.

"Safe? I don't know, but where else are we going to go? Are we going to sit in this garbage all day? Besides, my legs are starting to burn, I need to stretch," Jefrie said as he began to stand up.

As his head crossed the top of the crates, his heart sunk and he froze in place as the side door creaked open. Instinctively he ducked down, crashing into Arthur and nearly losing his balance. Arthur held him back from falling into the crates and both tried to become as still as the garbage.

"You trying to get us killed!" Arthur scolded.

Jefrie glared at his friend. "It wasn't my fault!" he began to argue, but then stopped as the door opened all the way.

Three figures exited through the open door. All were garbed in black robes that hung from their shoulders and an embroidered hood shrouded each head. Their presence demanded cowering and Jefrie felt the urge to walk out and kneel before them. *No wonder Tret was afraid* he thought as he felt a shudder tingle his skin.

"He should be here any moment," one of the figures said.

Jefrie and Arthur both gave a start, and Arthur mouthed, "We need to get out of here!" but Jefrie shook his head. If they moved now they would be discovered, and his instincts said if they were discovered, they would be killed. *What kind of mess has Uncle gotten into?*

"Do we really need to involve him, Dark Lord?" One of the other figures asked.

"The Chosen can handle it by ourselves, Dark Lord," a near identical voice said.

The first, who Jefrie now recognized as the Dark Lord shook his head. "We need to eliminate and contain this threat. At this point we can be sure the threat includes Tret, his wife, and the Master Dralchemist—Kloin. In order to contain, Morgar needs to be involved."

"We can handle it—"

"I have made my decision," the Dark Lord

interrupted, ceasing the argument.

Suddenly another figure appeared as if it had materialized out of thin air, giving Jefrie another start.

"Where did he come from?" he mouthed to Arthur, who shrugged his shoulders. Jefrie could see in his friend's freckled face that Arthur was having difficulty keeping his emotions controlled. *We have to get out of here soon!*

And then he saw it. The figure that had materialized was the only one not covered by robes, and Jefrie wished that it had been.

One side of the creature looked like a disheveled human, but as it turned toward its master, Jefrie saw the other side glimmering with scales that covered thick and powerful muscles that palpitated with every movement. Two half-mooned wings protruded from jagged shoulders, rising and falling as the creature breathed. And then Jefrie saw its face. A jagged snout filled with deadly incisors protruded from its face, covered in the same black scales that shielded half its body, leading to two human eyes that were filled with rage.

"Jefrie," Arthur whispered. "We have to get out of here, I mean, we are going to—"

Jefrie clasped his hand over his friend's mouth as the beast abruptly turned toward them. He felt Arthur become even more rigid, felt his friend's face bead with sweat as he held his hand tightly over his mouth. He could feel his own sweat pouring down his back, his legs screaming in pain from staying in a squat as long as he had. He could hear his heartbeat pounding in his ears. He was positive the beast could hear them; his heart was beating so loud.

"Morgar," the Dark Lord said.

The beast stared at them a moment longer before it turned back to its master. Then it bowed slightly as it said, "Morgar is here to serve, Dark Lord."

"As always," the Dark Lord responded. "We must act quickly. Tret Danglon identified us and we must contain any chance of this spreading. The Chosen will eliminate the threat of the Danglons, but you, my trusted Morgar, I need you to destroy a dralchemist."

"Dralchemist? Morgar despises dralchemists. Painful," the beast slithered.

"Yes, Morgar, painful will suffice. His name is Dard Kloin. Be careful. Though he is elderly, he is wily and very skilled at his profession. You," the Dark Lord said pointing to one of the Chosen. "Go with Morgar, clean up his mess as much as possible, the Danglons shouldn't require two of you."

"Morgar will not fail, Dark Lord."

"Then be gone," the Dark Lord commanded. "All of you."

With that, Morgar crouched into a squat and then

erupted off the ground, its powerful half-mooned wings beating in the air as it rose higher and higher before finally disappearing from view. A moment later, the two other figures seemed to disappear and soon the Dark Lord was the only one remaining. The Dark Lord looked after his servants and then turned back toward the door and disappeared inside.

As the door bolted shut, Jefrie finally let go of Arthur's mouth and they both stood slowly and quietly, neither willing to say anything that would confirm what they had just witnessed.

Jefrie's mind raced with possibilities as words coursed through his mind. Eliminate? Destroy? Contain? *What should we do first?* He felt powerless and lost.

"Jefrie, we need to get out of here before they come back," Arthur said, his voice still shaking with fear. "We need to hide. Or leave the city, or I mean —dragon's blood—what are we going to do!"

Jefrie shook his head. "Arthur," he said as he tried to calm his own unsteady voice. "We need to warn them."

"Warn them?" Arthur asked, his voice rising. "Are you serious? They are going to be murdered! We need to run!"

Jefrie looked around to see if anyone had heard them. For a moment he thought he saw the side door beginning to open again, but it stayed shut.

Mind tricks! He frantically tried to think of a way to calm his friend, but Arthur was close to hysteria. *I'm surprised I'm not.*

"We are going to die!" Arthur hysterically shouted.

Without thinking, Jefrie punched his best friend in the face, causing Arthur to stumble back and crash into the wall of crates. Arthur went down in a heap of rubble and trash, and then stood up with a look of fire in his eyes.

"What was that for?" he shouted, his eyes focused and determined.

Jefrie smiled. "There's the Arthur I know. The sworn protector of Master Kloin," he stated.

Arthur grit his teeth and opened his mouth to begin arguing, but then shut it, and then a smile appeared. "We've got to help," he declared.

Jefrie agreed. "Kloin's place is closer, let's try to get there first. Tret at least has a head start, and from the look on his face he knows they are coming. Kloin won't know until it's too late. We need to warn him."

Arthur unsheathed his dirk as he nodded in agreement. "Then let's go. Today I earn my keep."

If it was a different situation, Jefrie may have laughed at that comment, but instead they turned and ran out of the alleyway on their way back toward Master Kloin's.

* * *

Tret slammed the door shut behind him, bolted the locks, and then turned his back to the door and slid down until he rested on the floor. His breathing was heavy and his muscles burned. He had never run so far or so fast in his life.

"Tret? Is that you?" he heard a voice call from the kitchen down the hall.

He tried to gather his breath so he could respond, but instead just gasped again for air. *I'm not Jefrie! I'm not fit to run like that!* He reached for the door handle and struggled back to his feet as his wife walked into the hallway.

He smiled as he saw his beautiful wife enter the room. She was about four years younger than him, with only a single streak of silver touching her otherwise deep brown hair. She smiled back at him and again said something, but he couldn't hear her. The only thing he could hear was his heart pounding in his ears, and the only thing he could feel was a tremendous headache forming.

"Tret? What is going on? You look as if you've seen a dragon?" he heard her ask.

The memories of what had happened flooded back to him. He quickly looked back at the door and checked the locks. Satisfied they were how he left them, he tried to remove any emotion from his face and then slowly turned back around.

"We need to pack. And leave. Immediately," he said.

"What? What are you talking about, Tret?" Malline asked. "Are you feeling all right?"

"I'm feeling fine, but...there is no time to explain, Malline. We need to get out of here. And we aren't ever coming back. It's not safe."

At first Malline started to smile as if her husband was playing a cruel joke, but when Tret's face remained serious, she swallowed hard. "What is going on?"

"I saw something today, Malline..." he began as he looked back at the door, "...something that I wasn't supposed to see. Something...they are coming for me, I know it."

"Then let's call the guard. If someone threatened you, then they will deal with it. We'll go before Judge Scot, he'll set it straight."

"Malline, this goes higher than even Judge Scot. I can't explain it, and honestly I'm too afraid to even say it out loud! The one thing I know is they are coming for us! He pretty much promised that!" he said as he stepped forward. *If she's not going to listen I'll pack myself and force her out the door!*

As he stepped forward, his headache pounded to a crescendo and he felt the world spinning around him. He heard a crash as he lost his balance and stumbled onto the hallway floor, landing hard on his side, his breath escaping his lungs upon impact.

"Tret!" Malline exclaimed as she ran over. "Are you all right?"

Frustrated, Tret tried to right himself but the dizziness was too powerful, so he stayed crouched on hands and knees. *Dear Creator I am out of shape!* "I'm just tired. I sprinted straight from the Merchant District, and I fear that run may kill me before they do!"

Malline crouched behind him and felt his head. "You aren't running a fever," she stated.

"I know I'm not. I'm telling you, Malline, it's from the run. I just need a drink is all, and then once I catch my breath, we need to leave. It may be too late already!"

This time Malline didn't argue, and she stood up and disappeared into the kitchen, returning a moment later with a glass of wine.

Tret forced himself off the floor and crawled until he could rest against one of the couches in the room. Once situated, he tried to calm his breathing as Malline gave the glass of wine to him. He took it with trembling hands—*is the trembling from my fear or from my fatigue*—and brought the liquid to his lips.

The wine was cool and as it touched his tongue he swallowed quickly and in full. It cascaded down his throat and seemed to invigorate his body. He was not expecting the sensation and suddenly sat up straight, regaining his strength almost immediately.

"Malline," he said, his voice much stronger now. He could see from the look of surprise on her face that she was also confused by the sudden change in his appearance. "What is this wine?"

But then he tasted the tang of a plant he knew had only one purpose. He dropped the glass of wine and stared straight at his wife as the glass shattered on the wooden floor below.

"Tret, what is going on?" Malline asked, her voice thick with worry.

Tret knew his wife's concerned face was a reflection of his own. "Where did you get that wine?" he asked as calmly as he could, but each word seemed to tremble out of his mouth.

"A man had brought it just before you came home. He said it was a gift for the hard work you were doing," she responded. "Why?"

Tret swallowed hard, his fear growing stronger with each word that came from her mouth. He rubbed his tongue against some of the liquid that remained in his mouth and as it touched the wine, the astringency confirmed his suspicions. Kloin had taught him about this herb, about all the herbs of dralchemy, and as a result, Tret knew the signs of how to recognize them. He knew exactly what this herb was. Astercaea. The herb used to create dragonlyst.

"He told me that you deserved it and so he delivered us this fine wine," Malline continued. "I thought you would appreciate it…"

Tret just shook his head. He knew what this meant. "Did you drink any of it?" he asked.

Malline shook her head and Tret let out a sigh of relief. He quickly stood up, surprised at how much strength had returned, but then immediately discarded his surprise. *Dragonlyst does that* he knew.

"You need to leave, immediately," he instructed Malline as he grabbed her by the arms. She started to protest, but he pushed her toward the kitchen against her will.

"Tret, let go! You are hurting me!" she said, her voice now frightened. "What is going on?"

Tret started to feel his body growing stronger. He knew what that meant. He knew that dragonlyst had one purpose. It would either act as a catalyst in the transformation process, or it wouldn't. The way his body was responding so rapidly to the dralchom, he figured he knew what he would face.

"I'm trying to save your life," he said. Then he felt a fierce pain rip through his stomach and course upward. He let go of Malline and brought both hands to his abdomen, clutching it and trying to force the pain to go away. His stomach felt as if it were on fire, an intense and poignant pain. He gasped for air and then saw it. The source of the pain was deep within, a glowing ember starting to form against his will from somewhere deep in his abdomen.

"No!" he screamed as he forced all of his feelings toward the ember in an attempt to try to smother the growing pain. Suddenly the ember started to ebb, and began to disappear back inside.

"Tret? What is going on?" Malline asked in a trembling voice.

Ignoring her, Tret stood up, shocked that the pain had subsided and stepped forward. *I must act quickly! I must get Malline to safety!* Grabbing Malline by one arm he forced her to the back of the kitchen and to a door that led to an alley outside. He reached down to the handle and gave it a twist.

Locked.

Reaching down he unlocked the handle and then tried to open it again. The door wouldn't budge.

"What is going on!" he screamed. He tried to turn the handle again, but it wouldn't move. He kicked at the door, started pounding on it, and then finally decided he would break it down. Just as he lifted his foot to kick the door, the curtain of the window moved slightly. Tret almost lost his balance as he saw a man garbed in pitch-black staring at him through the window. The man's pale face was uncovered and his penetrating eyes stared right at Tret.

Tret recoiled in shock. He recognized the man from earlier that day—he was one of the thirteen.

Sudden realization registered as he comprehended the situation he was in. He almost had a sense of appreciation at how thorough they had planned, and how effectively they had implemented it—all with a touch of irony. He would be infected with dragonlyst and either transform and do the killing, or be killed by the one who stood guard. There was no escaping this night. He knew too much and it would die with him. *And they will force me to share this horror with my wife.*

He was surprised at the sudden calm that filled him. Turning to his frightened wife, he reached out a tender hand and grabbed hers, squeezing tightly to try to show comfort. As their eyes met, he smiled once before pulling her close and embracing her deeply.

"I love you, Malline. I am so sorry for bringing this upon you," he said.

"I love you too, Tret. What is going on? Who is that man? I'm scared. Are you ok?"

Not knowing where to begin and not having the time to explain, he tried to reassure her with a smile. A sudden ache in his side told him he only had a few moments remaining, a minute or two at best. With his mind racing he decided on two things. "Malline, go into the basement and lock the door behind you, and do not open it, no matter what you hear."

"What?"

"There is no time! Just promise me, please!" he yelled. He almost apologized as he saw the hurt on her face, but he knew this was the only chance of survival that she had. The pain was growing stronger and deeper. *There just isn't time!*

"Tret, I'm afraid!"

Tret tried to calm himself, but the pain was growing and becoming more intense. He looked straight into Malline's eyes and she stumbled back.

"Your eyes!" she said. "They're…Tret…are you all right! What is going on!"

Without saying a word, he picked her up and ran to the hallway, opened a door to the basement, and pushed her down a few stairs. "Lock the door!" he yelled.

The pain had moved from his abdomen to his chest and his entire body felt like it was on fire. He thought back to earlier and how he was able to control the pain by focusing on it. He searched within to try to find the source of pain. This time it was easier to find. Instead of finding a small ember, there was a raging furnace. *I am out of time!*

Running back into the kitchen, he was determined to finish his second task. He grabbed an inkwell and a pad of parchment that lay near the table, and quickly scribbled a note. Then he ran to the front room and into the entryway closet. Throwing out boots and coats, he finally reached the bottom of the closet and lifted up a plank of wood that concealed a hidden compartment. He shoved the parchment into the compartment and then stumbled back.

His body was on fire now, the furnace turning into a conflagration as it spread throughout him. He clawed at his eyes in an attempt to reach the source of pain and create an outlet for the fire to escape his body. Deep inside he could feel it. Growing. The pain was determined to destroy him.

"Tret?"

The pain subsided for a moment as he turned and slowly regained his senses. Long enough to see that he had moved to the middle of the room and had knocked over the couch and two lamps. Clothes and boots from the closet lay strewn throughout the room. And then…there…standing at the top of the basement stairs was his beautiful wife.

He looked at her beauty and almost smiled, but then the fire within exploded. He saw her blue eyes fill with fear; he heard a shriek erupt from her lips. He knew it was happening. It was time.

"No!"

Templar Darcstearn calmly set down his glass of ale as he felt the familiar tugging of a transformation begin. Unconsciously he began rubbing his black beard as he focused on the source of the feeling. The feeling seemed to massage his conscious, confirming that a transformation was occurring, and revealing enough emotion that he could pinpoint the location of the source.

"Did you feel it as well, Darcstearn?" a voice asked him from the side.

Darcstearn stopped stroking his beard and looked at his Seeker companion, Keist. He nodded.

"Then it's from the Rahiad line, we need to move," Keist reasoned.

Instead of replying Darcstearn only nodded again. He reached out his own senses and tried to feel out the other Templars, but felt nothing in return. *Seekers have their uses* he thought with a hint of jealousy.

"Are you ready?" Keist asked as he stood up, grabbing his staff and throwing on his white cloak.

Standing up, Darcstearn threw his dark cloak over his shoulders and touched the hilt of his draestl sword. "Let's move," he responded.

Together they each threw a silver coin on the table, and then turned to leave.

Time to protect.

By the time Jefrie could see Master Kloin's house, the faint light from the setting sun was emitting enough light to cast strange shadows through the street. He tried to stop a knot from forming in his stomach as he immediately noticed what was different.

"All the other homes have their lights stoked and lit," Jefrie said as he started to pick up his pace.

Arthur said nothing, but he had noticed the same thing. Jefrie thought he had heard Arthur mumble something under his breath, but he was too nervous to ask what.

As they came closer, the knot became more entangled and intense as his master's home came clearly into view. The house stood dark and eerily still. And then…there…

"The front door," Arthur said faintly.

Jefrie had seen it too. The door was open.

"Did we leave it open?" Arthur asked as he slowed to a steady walk. Though he was still holding his dirk in hand, Jefrie noticed that it wasn't held as confidently any more, or as high. *Like our Spirits.*

"I know I bolted it. I never forget to bolt it," Jefrie stated.

Together the friends stopped. Assuming the worse, Jefrie tried to think of what to do. He knew they couldn't stand out there, especially if Kloin was alive and waiting to be rescued! He quickly dismissed the optimistic thought. *If Kloin was alive he wouldn't leave the door open.*

"We better go look. Just in case, right?" Arthur

suggested.

Jefrie was at first surprised and then ashamed that it was Arthur who had made the suggestion to enter. *I'm just standing here like a scared little child.*

"Well? I mean if Kloin's hurt, shouldn't we help him?" Arthur asked. And then quieter, "but if that thing is in there…"

Jefrie knew he didn't need to answer Arthur's last statement. *If that thing is in there, we are as good as dead.*

"Let's go?" Jefrie said, though softer than he intended. He was proud that he was the first one to take a step forward.

"Wait," Arthur interrupted. "You don't have a weapon, let me go first!"

Jefrie held up a hand to motion Arthur to stop and without turning around he said, "Arthur, if you need to defend us with that dirk—we are both dead."

"Hey!"

"And besides," Jefrie continued as he reached one hand into the pocket of his cloak and fingered a single vial that rested there, "Master Kloin taught me how to defend myself."

"Fine," Arthur conceded.

Jefrie continued to cautiously approach the house. As he walked up the steps to the front door, he saw that the door wasn't open at all. Instead it lay broken in two—half still attached to the hinges on the wall, and the other half strewn in the front entryway.

"This isn't good," Arthur whispered.

Jefrie grabbed the vial in his pocket and pulled it out.

"What's that?" Arthur asked.

Jefrie ignored him as he unstopped the vial. *I need to be ready.* He knew what this could do. He wasn't exactly using this dralchom for its intended use, but he understood the dralchemy behind it. If he threw it, it would explode. *It is caged fire after all.*

Now fully into the front room Jefrie once again realized how quiet it was. The only thing he could hear was his steady breathing,—*I'm surprised I'm so calm*—and his footsteps as they walked along the soft wooden floor.

He assumed that the sun must have set by now as it was nearly impossible to see, even as his eyes adjusted to the dark. Knowing the layout of the house by heart, he silently walked over to one of the sconces and grabbed the unlit torch. A quick sniff confirmed that it was still doused in oil, so he grabbed the flint that lay in the sconce and readied to strike a flame.

"Do you think that's smart?" Arthur asked.

"We'd already be dead if that thing was still here," Jefrie responded while no longer attempting to quiet his voice. He was surprised how loud it sounded in the silent home.

"Shhh!" Arthur demanded as Jefrie struck the flint. After several strikes a small spark ignited the torch.

The room was immediately flooded with light. As soon as Jefrie's eyes adjusted, he scanned the room. The images poured into his mind and he wished he could douse the flame and take back what he was seeing. He knew he would never be able to erase this memory from his mind.

Blood.

Blood was everywhere.

He forced his eyes shut and tried taking a deep breath to calm his nerves. *Is…this…Master Kloin's?*

A sudden clang caused Jefrie to jump out and he quickly turned around, ready to toss the vial at his attacker. Instead of seeing an attacker he saw Arthur standing with his jaw dropped open, his dirk resting on the floor beneath him, and his faced filled with shock.

"What in the name of the Creator is going on!" Arthur screamed.

Jefrie could only swallow hard. "That thing," he said, surprised that his voice was as steady as it was.

"Where is Master Kloin!" Arthur asked quietly.

Jefrie was wondering the same thing. He glanced around the room. The couches were torn to pieces, the office door was broken down, and then he saw the bookshelf that concealed the hidden basement.

Oddly enough, it was still in place.

"Maybe he's downstairs hiding?" Jefrie hopefully asked as he stopped the vial and put it back into his cloak.

"It is still shut," Arthur agreed. "But if he's down there. I mean, what's this blood then?"

"Maybe it's that thing's? Maybe Kloin killed it!" Jefrie reasoned. Hope continued to grow within him as he ran over to the bookshelf. *It's starting to make sense!* Once there, he reached down to the fourth book from the left, fifth row from the bottom, until he found the book he was looking for. He grabbed *The Power of the Order* and pulled on it, hearing it unlock the latch that held the bookshelf in place.

Then he pushed on the shelf and it slid free. He reached into his tunic and pulled out the key to the door that led downstairs. As he inserted the key he realized the door was already unlocked. His fear started to return, but he fought it. *We don't always lock it.* With torch in hand, he opened the door and rushed down the stairs.

By the time he was completely downstairs, his confidence grew as the light from the torch cast upon the contents of the room. The vials and flasks were how he left them, unbroken and complete. The dralchom herbs were still sitting where they were supposed to be. The cauldron lay dark and cool, undisturbed. *But where is Master Kloin?*

"Master?" he whispered quietly. "It's me, Jefrie! That thing is gone! You can come out, it's safe now!"

He took a step forward, and immediately recognized a wet feel on his boot. Looking down to the floor he saw the same blood that littered the upstairs. *No!*

Carefully he took several more steps, noticing that this blood was slightly different. Whereas upstairs the blood was splattered in disorder, this seemed to be carefully collected in the middle of the room as if it was making a path.

Then Jefrie realized what he was looking at. *It is a path…where the beast dragged Master Kloin.* He followed the blood trail. The room wasn't that big, and after realizing what he was looking at, he knew exactly where it was leading him. Just on the other side of the cauldron, hidden from his current view, was where Master Kloin kept his personal study journal; which contained every experiment and dralchom ever created by Master Kloin.

Hope again renewed within Jefrie as he thought about where the path was leading. *Maybe they didn't drag him here after all? Maybe he crawled?* Jefrie wondered. He knew that his master would try to protect his history at all costs. That he would even go to great lengths—*even crawl while dying*—to make sure his journal was safe. He quickened his steps.

As he rounded the black cauldron, he finally found his master. Master Kloin was laying in a fetal position, cradling the black tome that contained his life's work. Jefrie almost called out to Kloin, but then his mind registered what he was seeing.

A pool of blood surrounded the still form of his master, coming from dozens of open wounds that looked as if they were formed by claws.

Jefrie felt his stomach turn and he quickly looked away before he became sick. He felt his emotions swirl, felt his eyes begin to burn with tears, and his breathing became heavy. He didn't know what to do. He wanted to break down and cry, but at the same time he knew he needed to leave. He needed to warn his uncle. *It's too late for Kloin, I was too late...*

But he also knew he couldn't just leave his master like this. Fighting his emotions, he looked for anything in the room that he could use to cover up his friend and mentor, but there was nothing. *My cloak will have to do* he realized. Carefully he took the dralchom out of his cloak and put it on a table near the cauldron and then took off his cloak and began to lay it gently over his fallen master.

"Did you find him?" A voice suddenly called out.

Without thinking, Jefrie dropped the cloak, grabbed the vial, and threw it toward the intruder. As it left his hand he recognized Arthur's voice, and was barely able to yell out "duck!" as the vial flew toward his friend. Arthur reacted in time, moving his head just enough to avoid the flying vial and a moment later the vial shattered against the wall.

"Are you filled with dragon's blood, Danglon? What are you doing!" an angry Arthur yelled.

"I was startled you idiot, give me some—" Jefrie started to explain, but then he cut off as a sick feeling enveloped him as he realized what he had done. That vial contained the dralchom dragonsfire. Consumed it would act as a reagent. But if it was given momentum and exposed to force...

"Run!" Jefrie yelled.

"What?"

Jefrie couldn't explain. He didn't know how much longer they had. He started to step away, but then glanced down at his master one last time. He noticed his master's face this time. Kloin's face was contorted in pain, and his eyes were still open. Jefrie shuddered as he looked into the lifeless eyes, but then he noticed something. *Those eyes are filled with determination.*

Jefrie felt his own source of courage and determination grow. Looking at his master, and then to the tome his master was protecting even in death, Jefrie decided one thing. *Master Kloin's work will continue on.* Reaching down, he pried away the fragile fingers and arms and grabbed the bloodstained tome. And then turned and sprinted.

Seeing the look on Jefrie's face, Arthur didn't argue anymore, and together they sprinted upstairs.

Arthur stopped to shut the door, but Jefrie yelled at him.

"Forget it, Arthur! This place is going to explode!"

Arthur didn't need to be told twice as he picked up the pace of his sprint.

As they reached the doorway, they heard a loud hiss like a massive intake of breath, and then felt an unseen force slam into their backs.

They flew out the door and crashed onto the cobblestones of the street outside as the home exploded.

Pieces of wood, brick, and glass started raining on them as they tried to regain their feet. Neighbors started coming out to explore what the explosion had been, and Jefrie saw some point to others, shouting to go get the Alderidon guards.

Jefrie noticed he was having a hard time standing straight, and a harder time hearing. *That blast was so strong!*

A hand on his shoulder startled him and he lashed out, but then another touched his other shoulder.

"Go!" Jefrie finally heard.

"What?" Jefrie asked. He turned and saw Arthur trying to get his attention.

"Go! I said," Arthur was screaming. "Give me that book so you can run faster. I'll handle this, go to your uncle!"

At first Jefrie clutched the book tighter, determined to protect it. But then he heard what his best friend was saying. For a moment Jefrie had completely forgotten about his aunt and uncle. Reluctantly, he handed over the journal.

"Go! Now! I'll explain what happened here, just go. There still may be some time!"

Jefrie nodded and then turned to leave. Trying to gain the strength to continue, and ignoring the horrific images that continued to replay in his mind, he started to jog down the street. *Only a few blocks away* he thought as he picked up his pace.

And then he finally registered the last thing Arthur had said. *There still may be some time.* Having seen what they had done to Kloin, Jefrie knew that was wishful thinking.

Malline recoiled in fear, shocked at what she was seeing. Tret lay huddled on the floor amidst the boots and coats, screaming in pain. At first she thought he had gone mad, as he had begun to claw out his eyes. But then he stopped, and the calm, confident, handsome face that represented the man she loved dearly stared back at her. But then his eyes had turned into a deep golden yellow, and when they looked at her...

She felt herself cry out as Tret began thrashing on the floor again. She tried to move toward him so she could comfort him, so she could hold him until he recovered, but his violent wailing kept her at bay. She forced herself to try to think, but the constant seizing from her husband stole her attention.

"Dear Creator," she started to pray. Suddenly Tret stopped shaking.

Tret rolled onto his stomach, his face down on the floor, and the only sign that he was still alive was the subtle rise and fall of his chest.

She stepped forward cautiously.

"Tret?" she whispered, taking one more step.

Tret remained still.

Gaining confidence she walked toward her husband, praying that whatever had happened to him had subsided, that whatever vile demon had possessed him was gone.

She placed an outstretched hand onto his shoulder but immediately pulled it away as her fingers touched his skin. His skin was as hot as fire.

"Tret?" she asked, her worry returning. *What is going on?* She thought.

Grabbing a discarded coat from off the floor, she covered her hand and reached for Tret's shoulder once again. As she connected, the heat was still prevalent, but she could at least maintain her grip, and she applied a gentle shake. *All I want is a sign that you are alive!*

Nothing.

She fell forward and tears began to flow freely as she cradled her husband. "Dear Creator! What am I supposed to do! Please save my husband!" she pleaded.

Nothing.

"I'm not ready for him to be gone! I love him!"

And then she noticed a putrid smell. Surprised that a smell had distracted her during her mourning, she realized just how powerful it was. *What is that smell?* She tried to find the source.

Looking throughout the room, she wondered if it was something that Tret had dragged in, maybe something from the outside. Then she looked at Tret. *It's him that smells, isn't it?*

Tret let out a breath of air and she was once again met by the same noxious, powerful stench. It grew stronger as her husband exhaled, and then faded slightly as he inhaled. This time she recognized it.

Sulfur.

She recoiled back, her heart pounding as she dropped the coat and tripped over a pair of boots that caused her to crash onto the floor. Fear filled her as she thought of what was happening. Memories came back to her from her childhood, memories she had tried unsuccessfully to erase.

She recalled them now. She remembered the elderly lady falling over in the street, clutching her stomach. She remembered bystanders running up to help to see if the woman was in need. And then she remembered the smell. As soon as the sulfur arrived, the people ran away.

Then she remembered what happened to the woman in the yellow dress moments after she starting reeking of sulfur. She felt a shudder ripple through her body as the memory flooded her and filled her emotions with fear.

"No!" she screamed out as she remembered every detail from her youth, and as she recognized the signs that were unfolding before her. *Tret is transforming!*

As the thought entered her mind it finally registered. Immediately her fear was tempered and her wits returned. She remembered back to her youth. Her mother had recognized the smell and they had turned and ran. Malline remembered looking back as the woman viciously transformed. She remembered what happened to the people who didn't run. Now she knew why Tret was trying to force her to leave. He knew what was happening. He was trying to save her.

I need to flee. Now!

Her mind raced as she tried to think of an exit.

She knew the back door was locked, and that mysterious character was standing outside as if he was guarding it. Quickly her mind moved to the front door. She pulled herself to her feet and deftly stepped by Tret, ignoring him as he lay still on the floor, and moved toward the door. She reached for the first lock and released it. Then the second lock. Having all the locks free, she reached down to the handle and rested her hand on it.

"Please open," she whispered softly.

As she twisted the handle it didn't budge. She pushed harder. Nothing. She started to scream as she exerted all of her force against the handle.

Nothing.

The thought to try to kick down the door crossed her mind, but she knew that she wasn't strong enough to even cause it to budge. She was trapped.

Turning back toward her husband, she slumped her back against the door and tried to prepare herself for what was about to happen. But then she remembered the last thing Tret had tried to have her promise to do. *Go into the basement and lock the door behind you* he had said. She replayed her husband's words again and again through her mind. The basement. It was her last hope.

Quickly she pushed off the door and ran toward the basement. *The lock isn't that strong, but it may be just enough!*

Then something ripped.

Though she tried to ignore it, her feet stopped moving and her body turned. Enthralled, she forced herself to watch.

As she turned to look at her husband, her mouth dropped open as she saw the transformation begin. Tret's head contorted backwards and crashed into the floor as he cried out in pain. His clothing started to shred as his flesh stretched thin until it finally tore as it transformed into golden scales.

It began with his chest and appendages. His hands lengthened as terrible claws suddenly grew out of his nails, turning into black blades of death. His arms broke in several places as he fell forward, only to catch himself with his new hands, his joints repositioning and enlarging. His arms and legs started to bulge as they grew, until they no longer looked human. Out of his boots tore two large feet.

Tret screamed out in pain as he fell forward on his chest, and out of his shoulders grew two large wings. They shot into the air with intense force, rising several feet and then unfolding to reveal the full length of the massive wings.

Simultaneously, a tail ripped out of his backside and unrolled as if it were a blanket. As the tail stretched across the floor, several spikes began bursting along the top of it, popping out one at a time until it formed a jagged spine. The spiky spine went the length of the tail until it led to three long spikes that formed the end.

Then it was quiet.

For a moment Malline thought that the transformation was complete. Despite the horror she had witnessed, she couldn't avoid the awe that she was experiencing. It was surreal to see her husband like this. Massive legs had replaced both his arms and legs. Two large wings rested against his side. A new-formed tail moved back and forth slightly above the ground.

She looked at his face, and her mouth opened wide. "Tret?" she asked, seeing his face as she had always seen. *It hasn't transformed yet!* She thought. *Maybe he's safe! Maybe he will revert back!*

But memories of the elderly lady returned to her and she remembered what would happen next. *The mind and face was always last.*

Suddenly Tret yelled out in pain as his face appeared to cave in, and seconds later a muzzle erupted from within. His mouth widened as the muzzle grew and filled with incisors along the perimeter of the large maw. A long, forked, pink tongue rolled out and flicked as it tasted the air. Then his ears fell back against the side of his head as scales rippled from within until they tore through the flesh and began covering his face.

Tret reared back as the head started growing. It

began near the ears, followed by the maw, and finally the face and eyes. Suddenly Tret's neck began to lengthen until it was several feet longer and his body enlarged until it was proportional to the head.

Finally, as a transformed dragon, Tret fell to the ground.

I'm just glad he's no longer in pain Malline thought sadly.

Then she remembered what the lady did next. Flashes of images coursed through her mind. She remembered what happened to those who didn't run.

Her feelings of relief vanished as instincts of survival took over. She started to turn back toward the basement door when Tret's eyes opened.

"Dear Creator," she said in disbelief. "Tret, your eyes. I still see you!" she said. It was a sickening sight, but despite staring directly at a dragon, and though they were tinted yellow, his eyes still looked like Tret's. She took a step forward.

But the eyes were in pain. She could see that they were yelling at her to flee. She took a step back. *What is he trying to say?*

Then she noticed his stance. Tret's dragon legs were in a small crouch, his head was tight to his chest, and his eyes were open and pleading. *He's trying to stay back* she realized. *He's trying to give me a chance to flee.*

She almost reached out to him until the eyes

glazed over and were replaced with anger…and hunger.

She screamed as the dragon launched toward her. She tried to step back, but Tret was too quick, and she crashed into the wall as the dragon connected with her. An intense pain on her left side forced her to look, and she saw her shoulder in the mouth of the dragon's maw, its teeth digging into her flesh. Shocked at seeing her body inside the mouth of a dragon, she tried to scream, but nothing came out. *I am going to die!*

The dragon let go, and as she looked at the bloody face—*that's my blood*—for a moment she saw the eyes of her husband return. The dragon stepped back a few steps, disbelief appearing in its eyes as it comprehended what it had done. The eyes were sad and defeated.

"It's ok, Tret, I know you can't help it," she said as she tried to reconcile her husband. *It's not his fault. I still love you.* She tried to tell him this, but as she opened her mouth, the words came out in mumbles. *Why can't I think straight?* Her head hurt, and it started to spin, faster and faster.

Through her dizziness she noticed Tret's eyes glaze over again. This time she knew the dragon wouldn't be able to control its hunger. Closing her eyes, she pictured her husband in her mind, thought of the memories they had made throughout the years, and said a quick prayer that it would be over soon. She welcomed the dizziness.

This time as the dragon connected with her, she couldn't contain her screams.

Templar Darcstearn stood in front of the only home on the street that had no lights lit. It was a small brick home on the edge of the Workers District, a nicer home by measure, on a nicer street. The brick home had a quaint porch with two rocking chairs. Just above the front door, hung a homemade sign that read "The Danglons". *Ah, the unfortunate* he thought to himself. He took a few steps toward the porch, trying to find out where exactly the feeling was coming from.

He reached out to his senses, and tried to feel Rahiad, the bloodline he was in tune with. He glanced at Seeker Keist, who stood at his side, his staff in hand.

"I can confirm it happened here. And from the strength of it the transformation must be complete. The darkness is never a good sign," the Seeker said.

Darcstearn agreed. While just before and during the transformation the feeling was intense, once complete it was more of a steady beacon that pulsated in his conscience. That only meant one thing—a new dragon had been born, and now it was waiting inside.

"Are you ready, Templar?" Keist asked as he clutched the tall black staff in his hand.

Darcstearn regarded his Seeker companion and nodded. For a moment he let his mind wander as he looked at his friend. They couldn't be more opposite—Darcstearn was average height and stocky in build, Keist was tall and slender. However, both were well equipped to deal with dragons. Darcstearn with his Templar training, and Keist with his Seeker staff. *Together we will take down this beast.*

"Shall we? It's only gaining strength while we wait," Keist stated.

Instead of responding, Darcstearn nodded. He turned his attention back to the brick home in front of him and took a step forward. Unconsciously his right hand rested on the handle of his draestl sword while the other tapped his draestl armor. Having felt both, he knew he was prepared. *Time to die, beast.*

Moving forward, he rested his ear against the door as Keist moved up beside him.

"Anything?" Keist asked.

Darcstearn heard nothing. He shook his head.

Keist shrugged his shoulders. "Well, they won't all be easy," he conceded.

Darcstearn agreed with his friend as he started to reach for the handle. He knew too well that if they had heard struggling they could have put the beast down easily. The transformations were never pain free, so arriving during the transformation or shortly after made easy work. *It's easy to defeat something that is in intense pain and distracted.* When they heard silence, they knew they faced a dragon that was recovering.

As he touched the handle it turned as if it was unlocked, but as he applied pressure to the door, it wouldn't budge. Looking at Keist he raised an eyebrow.

"Another challenge, but another one we have faced before," Keist said as he shrugged in response.

Darcstearn looked at his companion again, for a moment wanting to scold him for talking, but he kept his comments to himself. He knew Keist thought and prepared with his mouth, while Darcstearn thought and prepared with his mind. He agreed with Keist's logic. If it was unlocked, at least they had an element of surprise. Now the dragon will know they are coming.

He motioned to Keist that he would kick in the door and that they should be ready, and then held up his hand to count down. One, two, he stepped forward and kicked the door and it went flying into the room and landed in an entryway.

Together they rushed into the main room, Darcstearn with his draestl sword in hand, and Keist just behind. As they entered, they were greeted with silence and darkness. *An eerie silence* Darcstearn thought. A single candle flickered enough light to barely illuminate the room, but it was enough for them to see shapes of objects. They circled the room and observed everything. The closet door was open; coats and boots lay strewn across the room. One couch was overturned, and there...

"Oh no," Keist said as he saw the mangled corpse.

Darcstearn walked toward it carefully. Little remained, but it was his duty to check to see if it was alive. As he stood next to the mutilated body, he nudged it with his foot. Nothing. *I'm not surprised.*

"Did you see whose house this is? I knew I recognized the name!" Keist harshly whispered.

Not in the mood to guess, Darcstearn asked, "Who?"

"Tret Danglon. He works for the Order—helped plan all of our trade routes," Keist explained.

Darcstearn didn't need any more explanation. He knew what Keist was eluding too. The dragon form always enhanced your natural form. And he did know of Tret Danglon.

"They say he's brilliant," Keist continued to whisper. "Which means this dragon may be the brightest one we've ever met."

"I hope you are prepared to die," Darcstearn said dryly as he gripped his sword tighter.

"I'd rather not today," Keist said. "Let's just be careful."

Then stop talking.

Turning his attention back to the corpse, he tried to replay the events in his mind. The overturned couch was probably close to where the transformation had begun or completed, and the dragon had obviously been near the corpse. *But where is it now?* He wondered.

He stepped back and peered through the rest of the house. The hallway he stood in led to a small kitchen, and then there were stairs that led to an upper floor. From the looks of the stairs, the creature hadn't been close to them. None of the steps were broken, and there were several unlit torches sitting calmly in sconces. *The dragon wouldn't have been able to go up there without knocking those down.*

"Do you think it's in the kitchen?" he heard Keist ask.

Darcstearn didn't think so. The kitchen was only several feet away. Dragons were known to breathe heavily, and this one had Rahiad blood—*I would sense him.*

"It's too obvious. This one is laying in wait. I can feel him. He is close—but where?" he whispered back.

He gazed back around the room, searching for any clues. The front entryway and living room were ruled out. It might be hiding in the kitchen, but he figured it would have attacked by this point; after all, they would have made easy targets when their backs were turned toward it. Glancing at the upstairs one more time he wondered if maybe it had moved up the stairs. *If it was careful enough, it may have avoided the torches.*

"Do you think there is a basement or cellar?" Keist suddenly asked.

Darcstearn looked around. *It's a possibility.* Then he saw it. Immediately opposite the stairs leading to the upper floor was a door. At first he had thought it was a closet, but now he recognized it as a door. Scolding himself he stepped forward. *Of course there is a basement in this part of the Workers District* he said as he reached for the handle.

"Be careful," Keist warned.

As Darcstearn touched the handle he pulled his hand back quickly and fell into a defensive crouch.

"It's hot," he whispered. "Be ready."

Reaching forward more cautiously this time, his hand touched the handle again. He twisted the door open.

The door creaked as he slowly pulled it open toward him. Once open, he stepped carefully into the dark, his draestl sword leading the way. He took one step forward and carefully rested his weight on the first step. As the step supported his weight, he took another. *Where is this cursed beast?*

"Can you see anything?" Keist asked from behind

him.

It was pitch black in front of him. "It's as dark as a dungeon down here," Darcstearn stated. He knew he needed to be able to see. "Hand me the flint," he said.

"Are you sure? If the beast is sleeping, fire will surely wake it!"

"If it's outsmarting us and waiting for me to walk down there blind, I'll be dead before I can react!" Darcstearn said flatly.

Reluctantly, Keist reached into his robes and pulled out flint.

Darcstearn squinted until he saw a torch resting in a sconce and reached for it. A quick sniff confirmed that it had oil, so he brought it around to the Seeker. Keist struck the flint and the torch ignited.

Suddenly light filled the stairwell and Darcstearn and Keist both brought their hands up to shield their eyes.

"Now at least we can see," Darcstearn said as he started to turn back around.

Just as he was completing his turn, he caught something from the corner of his eye. At first he thought it was a shadow, or a trick of the light, but he was almost certain there was something amiss just above Keist. Startled, he stopped his turn, and gazed up.

"What is it?" Keist whispered.

"Don't move," Darcstearn tried to whisper. He couldn't be certain, but he thought he saw a claw just above the Seeker's head. With his eyes, he motioned for Keist to look up.

Just as Keist started to look above him, the dragon dropped from above and landed on Keist. Darcstearn watched in horror as he heard his friend scream and then disappear beneath the belly of the dragon.

Darcstearn tried to reach his friend, but the dragon used its tail to slam the door shut and Darcstearn ran straight into it. He heard another scream on the other side and a loud thud. "No!" Darcstearn yelled.

Frantically he tried to push on the door but the weight of the beast was in its way. Using the torch he glanced down at the basement and realized that there was no exit. *The cursed creature trapped me!*

His mind raced as he tried to think of what to do. Keist was strong, but without a Templar at his side, the Seeker would be destroyed. Taking out his sword, he began to hack away at the door in front of him.

Keist continued to move his head as the maw of the dragon tried to gain a grip on it. His body ached from the shear weight of the beast, and he knew several of his ribs, and maybe his left leg, were already broken. He lay pinned as the dragon's body straddled him. Only his right arm was free, and he used it to push aside the dragon's head as it continued to try to bite him.

Glancing to the side, he saw his black staff resting idly near the kitchen about three feet away. He knew if he could reach it, the dragonsbane infused weapon would at least force the dragon to recoil. *After the dragon tries to strike me I'll try for it!*

The dragon's maw came in to attack. Quickly he slammed the side of its head with his free arm as he moved his head out of the way. The dragon recoiled back and Keist reached for the staff. He fell short by several feet. *There is no way I can reach it.*

The dragon attacked quicker this time and he barely brought his arm forward, connecting his elbow on the dragon's head. The force of the attack caused his own head to hit the ground, and he felt it starting to spin. He knew he was lucky to be alive. The dragon was still suffering from some lethargy from the transformation, otherwise he would already be finished. *I can't imagine what ambush we would have walked into if this dragon was fully recovered.*

Dodging another strike, Keist's head crashed into one of the dragon's forearms and he felt his scalp tear against the strong scales and spikes protruding from the arm. Again the maw came at him, teeth bared. *I'm not going to last long.*

He thought of the other weapons he had. A draestl dagger was at his waist, but the dragon's legs were too tight around him and he knew he wouldn't be able to unsheathe it. The only chance he had was if he could reach inside his cloak and grab a vial of dragonsbane.

He could feel the glass vial lying in a pocket over his heart just inside his cloak. He prayed it wasn't broken from when the dragon dropped on him, and knew that it was his only hope. If he could somehow reach it and toss it at the dragon, the dragonsbane would inflict enough damage to let him at least get out from underneath the beast. *Maybe I could reach my staff.*

Then he felt an intake of breath.

It's preparing to breathe fire!

Keist shoved his hand into his cloak, knowing full well that he would be incinerated as soon as the air connected with the fire within the beast's mouth. He wasn't in draestl armor. *I have no protection against this.*

Alarmed, he searched for the vial in his cloak and his fingers finally found it. *Still intact!* He felt a surge of hope as he grabbed it and brought it to his mouth. With his teeth he pulled out the cork, and just as the dragon's mouth opened to release fire, Keist pulled back to throw it.

Immediately the dragon's mouth slammed shut

and its head attacked. At first Keist thought the dragon was going for his head and prepared himself to die, but then he realized the dragon's target. *It's going after the dragonsbane!*

Keist tried to dodge the attacking head, but his arm was already in an awkward position and the dragon connected. Keist tried to hold on tight to the vial, but the speed of the attack was more than he could handle and the vial fell harmlessly to the floor beside him. The dragon then shifted its weight and looked directly at Keist, its eyes ablaze with hatred, and a fiery mist once again began to form in its open mouth. *Darcstearn was right. Time to die.*

He saw from the corner of his eye the door breaking free as Darcstearn hacked at it with his sword, but there wasn't enough time. *Just save yourself Darcstearn, I'm finished.* He caught a glance of his companion, and they locked eyes. For a moment he felt pity for his friend. Rahiad was coursing through the Templar now. Keist could see hatred in his friend's eyes. He knew part of the hate was unavoidable because it was from Rahiad, but he could also see guilt in the Templar's eyes. *It's not your fault, my friend.*

Looking up he saw the heat continue to grow, and the fire begin to ignite within the dragon's bosom. Keist knew it would be over in a moment and he waited for the inevitable pain to come.

Suddenly the dragon's maw shut and its gaze went from Keist to the front door. Keist was first surprised at the maw shutting, but even more so as he saw confusion fill the dragon's features.

Then Keist heard someone curse. Confused, Keist tried to position his head so that he could see what was distracting the dragon. He saw a brown haired young man, roughly eighteen to twenty years old, standing in the doorway. The young man's clothes were torn and tattered, his handsome face covered in soot, and a look of defeat, shock, and confusion was splattered across his face.

Keist tried to comprehend why the young man was there at all, but then he noticed the way the young man looked first at him, and then at the dragon, and then at the dead remains on the floor. As he comprehended what was happening, his features grew more and more troubled. *He just returned home* Keist realized. *He's family!*

Panic filled Keist as he realized what was happening, confirmed a moment later as the dragon grunted and then stood up tall, its features changing from confusion to bloodlust. The dragon rose into the air, and its mouth opened wide.

Keist struggled to bring himself to his feet. His ribs ached, and as he put his weight on his legs, he almost tumbled over. *I was wrong, they are both probably broken!* He leaned on the wall as the dragon's form completely filled the hallway. Keist saw the fire forming.

Turning back toward the man in the hallway, Keist took a step toward him. "Run!" he yelled. He knew what was going to happen next. "Run!" he yelled again.

The young man stood still.

"Run!" Keist yelled as he tried to stumble toward him.

He heard the intake of breath behind him. He had hoped that the young man would turn around and flee, but instead he just stood still, his face in shock, his feet paralyzed.

Realizing his own legs were about to give out, Keist stopped, and turned back to face the dragon. It was surreal how slow everything was moving. *I have enough time to position myself perfectly.* He knew what he needed to do. He had made the choice years earlier when he had first joined the Order. He could either sacrifice himself, or watch as this dragon destroyed its own kin. He would never let that happen.

Standing as upright as he could, he stood defiantly as the golden glow grew deeper and hotter in the dragon's mouth. He felt a sudden rush of adrenaline, and he took a step toward the dragon, screaming in defiance of death.

The blast of fire hit him square in his chest. He

felt an intense pain envelop him as he was thrust from his feet. He flew through the air until he crashed into the wall, going straight through the wooden frames until he landed amongst the outer brick wall. His cloak ignited and every part of his body screamed in pain. He was surprised he was still conscious and wished that he wasn't as he watched the dragon land right next to the man near the doorway. He said a quiet prayer, wishing he could have done more. *I'm sorry boy,* he thought. *I tried to save you.* He knew it was for naught. As soon as a newly transformed dragon saw kin, it would do anything and everything to eradicate it. Keist closed his eyes, not willing to watch the consequences of his failure. *Dear Creator, please make it quick for the boy.*

He heard a flash of steel and hope filled him. *Darcstearn!* He remembered.

Opening his eyes, he saw Darcstearn standing between the dragon and the young man. With one hand the Templar held his draestl sword, and with the other he calmly pushed the young man to safety. Keist saw Darcstearn look his way, could see the concern on his friends face, and he tried to shake his head. "Finish it," he tried to say.

He doubted if Darcstearn could hear him or not, but the Templar gritted his teeth and turned toward the dragon. Then he attacked. The dragon looked up as Darcstearn charged, and swung his tail in the air toward his new prey. The tail swung high, and Darcstearn deftly ducked under it, bringing his sword up as he passed, and struck it into the exposed tail. The dragon roared out in pain as the sharp blade passed through the tail, scales and flesh falling to the scorched ground.

A sudden blast of fire erupted from the angry dragon, but instead of trying to avoid it, Darcstearn stepped into its path. The fire hit him directly in the chest, crashing into the black draestl armor and forcing Darcstearn to take a step back. Grunting, Darcstearn pushed against the flame and tried to step forward. The force of the fire was strong, but Darcstearn was determined. Keist knew that if Darcstearn could keep his balance, that the draestl armor would keep him safe, and soon the dragon would exhaust its supply of fire.

The fire raged on. Keist could see that the determination on Darcstearn's face was waning. He could see that his friend was starting to buckle under the strain. The Templar's legs were trembling, his boots slipping back. *How did this dragon have such a vast supply of fire?*

Then the fire from the dragon stopped. The dragon looked confused and it opened its mouth and tried to breathe fire again, but nothing came. It roared in frustration.

The Templar moved. Rushing forward, he

brought his draestl sword above his head and with both hands, threw it directly at the dragon. As the dragon realized what was happening, it tried to bring its wings up to begin flying, but the sword flew true. The draestl sword struck the dragon in the face, the strong, sharp blade cutting through skin and bone until it came to a stop. The dragon dropped to the ground.

Keist watched as Darcstearn stepped closer to the thrashing dragon. The building was completely ablaze. The Templar had to jump to the side as a portion of the upstairs erupted and fell in flames. *This entire place is going to collapse soon!* Keist knew.

But then Darcstearn was standing next to the dragon. He reached down and grabbed the hilt of his draestl sword with both hands and yanked on the sword until it came free. Raising it over his head, he swung it down on the dragon's neck and its head rolled free. In a moment the body began a rigorous transformation, scales disappearing as they were replaced with broken skin, until Keist saw the torn, tattered, headless remains of Tret Danglon lying still on the floor.

You did it Darcstearn he thought as he faded into blackness.

Standing outside, Jefrie held the folded piece of parchment tight in his hand. He looked at Arthur, who continued to motion that they should leave.

It wasn't that Jefrie didn't agree with Arthur—after all, whoever did this may still be around and just might connect Jefrie with his aunt and uncle—but he couldn't leave. He had first lost his master, and now his aunt and uncle.

Looking down at the piece of parchment, he slowly opened it and read the scribbled words once again. It was pure luck that he had even stumbled into it. The Templar had pushed him out of the way of the dragon—*Tret*—and he had crashed into the closet. The floor plank was already up and that was when Jefrie had seen the lone piece of parchment.

He remembered when Tret had built the compartment with him when he had just turned nine years old. He had been so excited at the time to have a place to hide things. Mostly used for treats Tret would smuggle for him, it became a secret the two had always shared—thier special place. *It finally came in handy*.

"What is that you keep looking at?" Arthur asked as he looked at the parchment.

Jefrie had to step out of the way as more Alderidon guards arrived, each bringing pails of water to try to put out the fire. For a moment Jefrie was distracted, watching the men work to contain the wreckage—it had spread to the two homes next door as well—but then he saw the Templars again.

"How many do you think there are?" Jefrie asked.

"What?"

"Templars. How many do you think there are? Why couldn't they get here sooner?"

"Jef," Arthur said as he reached a hand out to rest on his friend's shoulder. "There is nothing we could have done. Come on, let's get out of here."

Jefrie thought about arguing, but Arthur did have a point. There was nothing else to be done. He looked at the Templars one more time and then back at the note. He read it quietly to himself.

Jefrie, I don't have time. I'm afraid I drank dragonlyst, and from the feel of it, dragon is in my blood. It was planted because they came for me for what I discovered. They only know about Malline, and I'm afraid she will die with me. You should be safe, but be cautious—and don't trust anyone. If you get this, know that you can find answers from the Order of the Dragon. The person behind this—

The fire had scorched the remaining half of the note. Jefrie wondered who was responsible for this. His uncle knew, and thought it important enough to tell him about it. *Am I involved somehow?* He wondered. *Am I safe?*

He knew that he may never have answers to those questions, but he did know one thing. His uncle had left him a message, and he was determined to solve it. Whatever name his uncle had written down, he would discover who that person was. He wouldn't allow Tret, Malline, or Master Kloin to die in vain.

He looked back at the Templars and wondered again of their involvement. He saw the one he heard called Darcstearn—the one who had ended up killing Tret—standing in a corner. He looked troubled, and alone. *At least his Seeker friend is still alive.* For a moment Jefrie thought he would go and talk to him and thank him for what he had done, but the look on his face showed he didn't want to be disturbed.

Could I ever be a Templar? He wondered. He almost laughed at the thought of it. Running around killing dragons with his bare hands. He knew what his place would be. His skill was dralchemy. The Order had been after Master Kloin for years, trying to get him to join so that he could share his wealth of knowledge.

Feeling the black tome nestled under his arm, he realized that he now had that wealth of knowledge. *Kloin always said I had as much skill as him* he thought. *Time to prove it.*

"I'm going to join the Order of the Dragon and become a Master Dralchemist," he stated. Ignoring his friend's gaping mouth he began walking toward the Order. For a moment he thought to turn back and look at the remains of Tret and Malline's house one more time, but he decided against it. *There is no time to mourn the past. I begin solving this mystery now.*

Read on for an excerpt from

DRAGON BORN

BOOK ONE OF
THE DRAHIAD CHRONICLES

PROLOGUE

MYSTERIES IN THE DARK

After banishing them for what we hoped was all eternity, and watching the portal close off behind them, I couldn't help but wonder if someday I would see them march back through, their brilliant red armor catching the light of day, and knowing all too well that they had returned to finish what they had begun...total domination...

SHADOWS FLICKERED ACROSS the open book as he delicately turned a thin, aged page, the words coming alive as the candlelight caught their darkened ink. He glanced at the words scrawled across the brittle parchment, and although the words were chiseled into his memory, he still read it aloud.

"A cup of blood, the red knight adorn, the key to both, the white dragon reborn. The red knight lives, the red knight dies, but the return of the red, herein the blood lies."

He felt the familiar frustration begin to develop

within his conscious, anger stirring over the complexity of the riddle. He wondered if he would ever solve it. Glancing at the entire tome, he thought of the several hundred riddles he had already solved. Some of those had been difficult as well so deep down he knew he could solve this one, but he had been telling himself the same thing daily for the better part of a decade.

He read the words again, this time in a soft whisper, hoping that perhaps if he changed the inflection of his voice that it would be key to solving the riddle. "A cup of blood," he began, but then stopped. That was the last piece he needed to solve. What was the cup of blood? Was it related to the end of the riddle, where herein the blood lies? Was it the blood of the dragon? The Rahiad? The Vahiad? Was it human blood? Bloodheim blood? The questions continued to inundate his mind, questions he had asked more than a thousand times, but still questions without answers.

Feeling the anger beginning to boil within, he abruptly stood up, carefully set the ancient tome on the weathered maplewood table, and stretched his arms above his head. The library was dark at this time of night. The only light was emanating from his lone candle, which was casting eerie shadows on the overstuffed shelves filled with tomes, books, manuscripts, and scrolls.

The candlelight caught his eye and for a moment he wished it would extinguish. After all, the Dark Lord found comfort in darkness.

He noticed that the wick of the candle had about a quarter left—not that he was surprised. This was the routine of his life. Every night, he would come to the abandoned library, alone, with the sole intent of solving this remaining riddle.

For a moment he felt his mind drift to when he first came across his treasured tome. Buried in the labyrinthine library, he accidentally stumbled upon it when searching for something else entirely, but as soon as his eyes connected with the abysmal black leather cover, he felt it calling to him. He remembered clearly the first time his fingers had touched its cover. He had felt the innate power of the book immediately permeate his outstretched hands, and as he read the first riddle, he had felt the magic of it encapsulate his mind and soul. *The Book of Dragons*. The lone manuscript that wrote the truth of their heritage and prophesied the way to return the rightful rulers of Ardonor.

It was only a short time after his discovery of the tome that the dreams began. He felt a tingle form at the bottom of his spine and slowly begin to rise, filling his body with a sense of wonderment and fear as he remembered that first encounter.

A tall figure had appeared in his room, covered in

a brilliant crimson red robe with a hood that covered an elongated head. He watched as the figure approached and could feel a power emanate from the being as it walked to his bedside. He tried grasping for air—realizing that he was holding his breath—but the power to control his body was paralyzed by the presence of the visitor.

The hooded figure stopped at his bedside and pulled back the crimson hood that concealed the person's face. He recognized the person immediately—though he had never met him. The figure was Lord Soren.

The stories had said that Lord Soren was a powerful elf that stood over twelve feet tall. That he had ashen skin comprised of scales and that he possessed crimson eyes that had the power to paralyze just by looking. Beholding the Lord of the Bloodheim now, he knew the only exaggeration was the height.

A soft breeze caused the flame of the candle to shift violently, momentarily forcing the room into darkness before reigniting. He was grateful for the disruption in his thoughts. He didn't like to remember what happened next. The vow he had made; the turning point in his life.

The Dark Lord sat back down in his wooden chair and touched the tome once again, feeling its power seep into his body. "If I'm to serve the

Bloodheim, why is this riddle impossible to decipher!" he said in disgust.

"Riddles? Morgar loves riddles," a voice spoke from the dark.

He stood up quickly, a draestl dagger appearing in one hand as he summoned the feeling of rage within his bosom. He felt his senses enhance, the somewhat dark room brightening as his eyes adjusted, and he turned around so he could smell and sense the source of the voice. Then his mind registered the words that were said, and he relaxed, recognizing the voice and the name.

"Morgar," he said calmly as he sheathed his dagger and sat back down. "Come out from behind those shelves. You shouldn't be here, or be observing me."

He watched as a foot stepped around the bookshelf. Instead of seeing a shoe, he saw five gnarled toes, some with unkempt claws protruding from the end, others with human nails. The foot was covered in small scales that were hardened armor. Then the second foot stepped out, this one covered in a shoe, and he knew a human foot could be found within.

"Dark Lord," the creature slithered as he stepped out from his hiding place, a forked tongue flicking in and out of his mouth.

The Dark Lord looked at the creature Morgar.

The feet were only an omen of what the entire creature was. One leg was naked and covered with thick black scales and chiseled muscles. The other leg had what appeared to be the remnants of a pant leg covering an equally muscled human leg. When he glanced at the torso he saw a powerful abdomen and oversized chest fully covered by black scales. He watched as the creature breathed in and was amazed that the scales didn't rip since it was so tight against the rippling muscles.

Next he saw two arms carefully positioned by Morgar's side, his right arm covered in black scales that lead to a massive hand with jagged claws. His left arm was completely human and wielded a draestl sword, the blade stained red.

Morgar's shoulders were broader than any human, several feet wide and a half-foot deep. Along the top of the shoulders spikes ripped through the black scales, and protruding from the back of the shoulders were two half-mooned wings.

He glanced into Morgar's eyes. The eyes and left side of his body were the last remnants that even hinted that Morgar had once been a human. A massive snout that had torn through his mouth overwhelmed the rest of this face. Instead of seeing pearly white teeth when the creature spoke, there were gray triangular teeth interlocked with one another to form rows of incisors, capable of cutting through bone.

"Dark Lord," the creature slithered. "Morgar is here to serve. Please do not punish Morgar. Morgar is but a humble servant."

Annoyed that Morgar had come unannounced, and more annoyed that it was in the library, the Dark Lord allowed the thought of killing Morgar to cross his mind. After all, Morgar was merely an experiment gone wrong. He was intended to be a perfect hybrid. Gaining the strength and mind of a dragon, but maintaining the form of a human. But instead of a perfect hybrid, they had produced a half turned monster—one he called a dragonling.

"You shouldn't have come unannounced," he repeated. "Especially during my studies."

"Apologies, Dark Lord, please, have mercy. Morgar will make it up to you. Morgar always does."

The Dark Lord nodded. *Yes, Morgar, you always do.* Morgar had quickly proven himself to be his most dependable and trusted asset.

"I will let it pass," he told the monster, "but only if you leave me at once!"

Morgar obediently turned, but then stopped and turned back. "Dark Lord, Morgar has one question."

For a moment, the Dark Lord felt his adrenaline rise at being disobeyed, but then he saw the curious look in Morgar's human eyes. As if Morgar knew something.

"What is it, Morgar?" he asked. "Make it quick!"

"You always stare at the book, yes, Morgar watches you, though Morgar knows Morgar shouldn't. But every night Morgar sees you do this. Morgar wonders why?"

The Dark Lord's curiosity was peaked. Morgar was perceptive; he had proven that much in his service. *Could he discover an answer to my riddle?* He immediately discarded the thought, knowing that it was only his hope of solving the riddle manifesting itself.

"It's a riddle," he still found himself answering.

Morgar jumped up as his wings began to beat excitedly.

"Oh, tell Morgar, Dark Lord! Please tell. Morgar loves riddles, and is very good at solving riddles. He is the best there is at riddles. Oh yes, please tell!"

"I have been studying this riddle for years, Morgar, it is complicated," the Dark Lord replied. But again, he couldn't help but wonder if having someone else look at it would result in finding something he was missing.

"Morgar great at riddles, Dark Lord. Please tell."

"That is enough. Now leave me be," the Dark Lord commanded. *My frustration is having me depend on a half human dragonling—how desperate am I?*

"Dark Lord, please! Morgar will solve riddle. Morgar knows riddles."

"I said enough!" the Dark Lord demanded, his glowering eyes communicating his displeasure. He stood up quickly, and felt a surge of emotion develop within his core.

Morgar cowered back, raising his arms as shields as he groveled on the floor.

As the Dark Lord stepped forward, he could feel his senses enhance and felt the power begin to course through his body as it generated deep in his core. He looked at the dragon and focused his emotions into one feeling, causing the power to grow. His body began to fill with rage as the emotion built, his senses growing stronger and more powerful as he channeled. *I will not be disobeyed again!*

But then he noticed the sincere look in Morgar's eyes. *Morgar isn't challenging me; he's trying to help me.*

"Very well, Morgar. I will read the riddle," he said, feeling the rage leave and his senses normalize.

Morgar used his wings to push himself back to his feet, his hands clapping in excitement. "Thank you, Dark Lord. Morgar will not disappoint. I promise!"

The Dark Lord ignored the dragonling's promise as he sat back down and placed the tome in front of him. He enjoyed the feel of power as he touched its cover. He glanced at the riddle and then recited it out loud.

"A cup of blood, the red knight adorn, the key to

both, the white dragon reborn. The red knight lives, the red knight dies, but the return of the red, herein the blood lies."

He studied Morgar as the dragonling contemplated the riddle. "A cup of blood, that is tasty to Morgar," he said. "But not a real cup of blood, no. The red knight is the Dark Lord's master, the Bloodheim," he continued to reason.

The Dark Lord nodded his approval as he watched the dragonling decipher the riddle. *Yes, Morgar, the Red Knight is the Bloodheim.*

"This is a prophecy of the Bloodheim's return, yes Morgar, you are right," the dragonling continued. "The key to the return is the White Dragon. White Dragon I have seen before, yes very powerful, very key."

"None of which I haven't already solved, Morgar," the Dark Lord said, growing slightly impatient. The dragonling was only solving the obvious parts to the riddle. His impatience grew.

"Now its time to leave, Morgar, you haven't helped me at all."

Morgar spun around, his teeth bared and ears flat. For a moment the Dark Lord sat further into his chair, his free hand moving from the book to his draestl dagger. *Is the dragonling going to attack me?*

"Morgar not finished, Morgar will solve riddle!" and then the dragonling turned back around, muttering under his breath.

The Dark Lord looked at his dragonling, thinking for a moment to force the creature out of his presence, but again saw the devotion in the dragonling's behavior as it searched for an answer to the riddle. He couldn't punish Morgar for his diligent obedience, his unquestioned loyalty, and his overwhelming desire to serve. *I will tolerate this for a moment longer.*

Morgar continued to mumble under his breath as he began to pace back and forth. Occasionally he lifted his head with excitement, only to lower it in frustration a moment later.

The pacing continued until the candle began to flicker as the wick reached its end. With a sigh the Dark Lord stood up. He felt sincere disappointment as he realized that he had been hoping Morgar would solve the riddle. *This riddle will never be solved.*

"Come Morgar, we'll revisit this riddle another night," he said as he picked up the candle and turned to leave.

"A cup of blood is the Chalice of Fire, Dark Lord. Yes, Morgar is correct."

The Dark Lord heard a gasp and then a loud clang as the candle he was holding suddenly hit the ground. The library flooded into darkness and he felt his heart beat rise, his senses kicking in immediately.

"Yes, Morgar, that makes perfect sense. You are correct," the Dark Lord said in astonishment. Together they had solved the riddle. He knew what that meant. *The Bloodheim will return.*

ABOUT THE AUTHOR

Randall Seeley currently lives in the midwest with his wife, three sons, and little girl. When he isn't acting out grand adventures and battles with his children, his hobbies include photography, hiking, and anything to do with the beach. He's had a passion for writing since he was a very young boy and *Dragon Born* will mark his debut novel. Find out more about Randall Seeley by visiting his website:

www.randallseeley.com

OTHER BOOKS BY RANDALL SEELEY

THE DRAHIAD CHRONICLES
Dragonlyst - A Short Novel
Dragon Born (coming Spring 2014)

CONNECT WITH ME:

Follow me on Twitter:
https://twitter.com/Randall_Seeley

Like my page on Facebook:
https://www.facebook.com/randallseeley

My Website:
www.randallseeley.com

Made in the USA
Charleston, SC
18 March 2014